Willow and the Snow Day Dance

by Denise Brennan~Nelson

Illustrated by Cyd Moore

For Mrs. Dubay, who taught us the snow day dance and so much more.

And to Jane, Kim, and Allie, thank you!

—Denise

For my luminous friend, Amy.

—Cyd

Text Copyright © 2011 Denise Brennan-Nelson
Illustration Copyright © 2011 Cyd Moore

Sleeping Bear Press™
315 E. Eisenhower Parkway, Suite 200
Ann Arbor MI 48108
www.sleepingbearpress.com

Sleeping Bear Press is an imprint of Gale, a part of Cengage Learning.

Printed and bound in the United States.

10 9 8 7 6 5 4 3 2 1

Printed by Bang Printing, Brainerd, MN, 1ˢᵗ Ptg., 11/2010

Library of Congress Cataloging-in-Publication Data

Brennan-Nelson, Denise.
Willow and the Snow Day Dance / written by Denise Brennan-Nelson ; illustrated by Cyd Moore.
p. cm.
Summary: When Willow's family moves to a new home, she makes friends with all of the neighbors, even unsmiling Mr. Larch, through her letters inviting each to be as generous as she is.
ISBN 978-1-58536-522-7
[1. Neighborliness—Fiction. 2. Generosity—Fiction. 3. Moving, Household—Fiction.] I. Moore, Cyd, ill. II. Title.
PZ7.B75165Wis 2011
[E]—dc22   2010030381

r. Larch never had visitors. Not even on holidays.

Only the mailman had a reason to approach the gray house known to the neighborhood kids as The Cave.

On the rare occasion when you might catch a glimpse
of Mr. Larch, he was stooped over, twisted and knotted
like an old apple tree.

And he always wore a hat. But he never wore a smile.

His yard was lifeless. No flowers in the spring or summer. No birdhouses or feeders. In the fall months, when yards were decorated with pumpkins, scarecrows, and ghosts, Mr. Larch's yard was bare.

And in winter, Mr. Larch posted signs that made it clear to the neighborhood kids there would be no sledding on his hill.

Across the street in a canary yellow house with turquoise shutters and a cherry red door, a little girl and her family were moving in.

Willow loved her new house and neighborhood.

A tire swing hung from the sycamore tree in the back yard. There were wide sidewalks, a basketball hoop, and a place to plant a garden.

Behind the quiet grey house there was a hill. Willow imagined it frosted in snow like a vanilla cupcake. It would be the perfect hill for sledding.

It was early spring and Willow couldn't wait to start gardening.

Willow helped her mom clean out the flower beds and dig up a sunny patch of lawn for a vegetable garden.

They had brought plants and clippings from their other house but there was room for more.

Dear Neighbors,
I am planting a garden, and in need of all types of seeds and seedlings. Can you help?
Your friend and neighbor,
WILLOW

Her generous neighbors kept Willow and her mom busy all spring!

Before long, summer arrived.

Everyone admired Willow's garden! The birds and butterflies, even the deer enjoyed the colorful plants and flowers Willow and her mom had carefully planted, mulched, and watered.

Willow cut flowers from her garden and made bouquets to share with her neighbors, even Mr. Larch.

Dear Neighbors,
Thank you for all the plants!
I especially like the sunflowers.
Claude Monet would be proud.
Your friend and neighbor,
Willow

P.S. I am looking for scraps for my garden art projects~ Can you help?

In autumn, Willow shared vegetables from her garden with her neighbors, even Mr. Larch.

The annual hat and mitten drive was underway at school, and once again Willow's request for help was answered.

Dear Neighbors,
Thank you for all the mittens, hats and scarves! The charity drive at my school was a big success! Lots of heads and hands will be warm!
Your friend and neighbor, Willow

Winter was just around the corner. Every night,
Willow fell asleep thinking of all the things she
would do when it snowed.

Best of all, when those soft, white crystals fell
from the sky, there was always the possibility
of a snow day.

Willow helped her dad get the winter boots and coats out of the boxes in the attic and wax the sleds and saucers. Now all she needed was snow.

She waited and waited and waited. But the north winds didn't heave a sigh, much less blow. Day after day went by and still no sign of snow!

One day, Willow overheard the teachers discussing the unusually warm weather.

"How long will our luck hold out?" said one to the other.

"I heard we're not supposed to get any snow all winter," was the reply.

As soon as Willow got home from school she wrote
and delivered another letter to her neighbors:

Everyone laughed at Willow's request. Well, almost everyone. The next day Willow found a mysterious note in her mailbox.

The Snow Day Dance

When the weatherman is predicting the chance of precipitation, follow these directions:

Before going to bed put your pajamas on inside out and backwards.

Tape a penny to your door or put a spoon under your pillow, whichever you prefer.

Get up on your bed and do a dance. The sillier, the better!

Get your family to do it with you. The more people that participate, the better!

A dance to make it snow? Willow couldn't wait to try it.

A few days later, Willow heard the weatherman predicting "winds out of the north and the slight possibility of snow."

She made copies of the Snow Day Dance instructions and took them to school to pass them out to every student and teacher.

And when Willow got home she left the instructions at every house in the neighborhood!

That night, she taped a penny to her door,

put a spoon under her pillow,

and with her pajamas on backwards and turned inside out

Willow did the silliest dance she could.

And she wasn't the only one...

When Willow woke the next morning she ran to her window.

Written in the snow, with snowballs of all shapes and sizes, sparkling in the early morning light, were those magical words, "Snow Day!"

And behind the houses, on the perfect hill for sledding (where the "keep off" sign used to be) wearing a stocking cap and the biggest smile you've ever seen...

was Mr. Larch!